Night Shift
Book One

M. D. Dalrymple

This story is first in the Men in Uniform series, about the men and women in blue, the brotherhood that serves and protects, and those who love them.

I would ask that, after you finish the story, please leave a review on Amazon or Goodreads:
https://www.goodreads.com/author/show/17969353.Michelle_Deerwester_Dalrymple).

Reviews are lifeblood for authors, and your reviews can help. Thank you!

One

There is no better moment for the lover of a police officer than the sound of Velcro separating. That harsh scrunching noise of the bulletproof vest coming off as officers undress in the bedroom both soothes and excites. That sound announces they are home; they are full of life, and many times, they are ready for the bedroom.

"No, down, down!" Officer Matthew Danes hollered to his beat partner, Ramon Garza.

Someone in the D.A.'s office fucked up, and now it was the butt-crack of dawn, and a meth dealer was waving a large rifle around a slummy neighborhood trying to rise above the title of ghetto. Danes eyed a pink tricycle and a jump rope abandoned in the grass at the house next door, surrounded by a worn chain-link fence, a feeble attempt to stop the vile nature of the street from infringing on the young family in the small, green house. The family had the misfortune of living next to a repeat meth dealer, a neighbor who tainted the imagery of childhood on the lawn. Now the fucker's decision would ensure him a return trip to prison.

"Dammit," Officer Danes cursed under his breath.

He and Garza squatted near their cars. The other cop was close to Matthew's own age, proud of his Mexican heritage, and one of Matthew's closest friends. Officer Danes did not want to see his friend's head blown off this day.

Matthew gestured to Garza, miming with his hands that if Garza could distract the meth dealer, then Danes would work his way around the back of the vehicles and driveway bushes and taze the perp while his rifle was raised. Garza nodded, his solemn face sweaty in the early morning heat.

When the meth dealer turned to evaluate the possibility of a run down the side street, Garza crept over to a large shade tree in the front yard, avoiding the thick, creeping roots that peppered the dead grass. Garza positioned himself against the tree trunk, his gun aimed at the dealer as Danes leveraged his own shotgun across the hood of the black-and-white and held his taser in his right hand, the sweaty perp in his own crosshairs.

"Hey, dumbass! Police! Drop your weapon!"

Garza's strong voice carried across the yard, and as the meth dealer swung his gun around, his eyes searched frantically for on the source of the voice.

Matthew found his moment, when the dealer's front was exposed as he spun, and fired. The meth dealer's body snapped backward, twitching upright for a moment before crumpling in a chaotic spasm in the miserable excuse of a yard. Matthew's eyes flicked back to the house next door, the children's toys an alarming contrast to the violence on the other side of the chain-link fence, and he could almost see the for sale sign up in the yard.

No one with a family would want to live in that house after all this.

Garza and Matthew fought over who would have to take the perp to jail and write the full report, and who would write the supplemental. Garza lost. Matthew banged out his paperwork in less than an hour, waved a cheery goodbye to Ramon, who flipped him the bird, and drove to his lonely bungalow one town over.

On days like this one, the welcome arms of a good woman were a more than a desire, they were a burning need, one that caused a deep ache in Matthew's chest as he tried to fall asleep in the dappled light of his bachelor pad. Rest, however, rarely came easy.

Nights like that night caused morning insomnia. Loneliness was not always a way of life for Officer Matthew Danes. As a ten-year veteran of the Tustin Police

Department in Southern California, Matthew spent the first five years of that time married. Living the dream, or so he thought.

His wife, however, had not appreciated the sound of bulletproof vest Velcro, or him. Always busy, too tired, or out running errands, she did not seem to want to be around him. He often ate dinner before work alone and found the bed empty when he came home exhausted from his 10-hour shift. Date nights had dwindled to silent dinners spent staring at phones. He tried to tell himself that he was not surprised when he learned she was having an affair with the bartender at the restaurant where she waitressed, but learning the truth of it still hurt his heart.

And the divorce was more brutal than it needed to be. She wanted more and more of his money, his investments, his pension, and dragged him through three years of divorce court misery. Ten thousand dollars later, the court finally dissolved the marriage, and his now ex-wife ran off with his money and her new man. Matthew had not heard from her in over two years, but sometimes his brain still spun in dizzy circles when he thought of it all.

He did not recover well. Even two years later, he guarded himself. He had dated a few women, usually blind dates set up by well-meaning brothers in blue, but he could not open up. Or perhaps he didn't want to open up. His heart still bore far too many raw scars to begin a relationship, and the guilt over dating women he would not have a second date with hounded him. He stopped accepting blind dates almost a year ago.

❖ ❖

The heat from the morning sun broached his blackout curtains. He tossed the sheets off his sweat-soaked body and rolled over to his other side. His tired brain tried to turn off the miserable march of his memories, but it was like an unending military offensive. He pressed his hands against his eyes in protest.

Then, to top it all off, his best friend and partner in life, Duggo, a huge German Shepherd/Rottweiler mix, stopped eating shortly after the divorce, and the visit to the vet showed invasive stomach cancer. Matthew put down the only foundation in his life amid gulping, sloppy tears. At least he could hold Duggo as he said good-bye. The idea that Matthew could have been at work when Duggo breathed his last doggy breath struck a painful chord.

Matthew blinked back sandy tears as he tried to work through the past seven years of sadness that weighed on his fleshy chest.

Now in a house by himself, no family, no wife, no dog, Matthew felt like he was the main character in a sappy country song. Frozen dinners and old reruns became his normal schedule, and he noticed he was putting on some unwelcome weight — not the life partner he was looking for. Grimacing over the new-found pudge on his belly, Matthew made a decision. He needed to bring this pity party to an end. He needed a significant change. When he was a Marine, he went on daily runs, and he was skinnier than a rail. While running may not give him the body he had fifteen years ago, it would go a long way to eliminate of some of the flab. And maybe regain some of his self-worth as well.

Having a moment of resolution, his eyes calmed, his brain settled, and his breathing fell into a steady cadence as he finally fell asleep.

Two

Before work that evening, Matthew popped into the sporting goods store not far from the station. The overly helpful teenager in the shoe department ensured Matthew tried on every size 11 running shoe they had, and Matthew left the store with a bag containing a sleek pair of black and yellow trainers, specialty socks, and a new pair of running shorts. Considering his state of mind over the last several months, he was impressed with his purchases. Other than his frozen dinners and coffee, Matthew had not purchased a single item for himself in years. When you sat in front of the TV alone, you didn't need a whole lot.

Feeling invigorated, he strolled into the locker room of the East Station. His recent mental change must have shown on his face, because Garza commented in the way only old friends can.

"Hey shitface. You look a lot less crappy today! What's going on?"

Matthew flipped him off as he opened his locker. "Shut your pie-hole, Garza. I look the same."

"No, you don't, brother. For the last few years you seemed to have your own personal raincloud above your head, but today, I dunno. It's like you have an umbrella up, or a wall. Still raining, but not drowning in it."

Matthew rubbed the back of his neck. Garza was right, as much as he hated to admit it. He was almost embarrassed at how long he remained in his rut. Even his friends could see it? Not good. Lost in his own thoughts as he pulled his shirt over his head, he wasn't ready for the cold slap on his belly.

"Shit, brother! When is the baby due?"

"Fuck, Garza. What's eating you today?" Matthew's anger was slow to rise, but Garza was like the heat under Matthew's tea kettle.

"Your sister!" Ramon actually clapped his hand on his knee at his own joke. Then his face fell into a serious mask. "No, really man. I'm worried about you. You are normally so tight, working out every day, a smile on your face. I know you've had a rough couple of years, but it's starting to wear on you. Do you need help, brother? Can I do something?"

The joking side of Ramon melted into concern. He hid sappy emotion with comedy — always the class clown — but he was sincerely worried about Matthew.

Matthew tipped his head to Garza. "Aw, brother, you do care!" He made to hug Garza in sweeping embrace, and Garza knocked his arm away.

"Really, though," Matthew continued as he zipped up his uniform shirt over his regulation white tee. "You are right. I've been in such a rut, not in a good way. Not just Erica leaving, but the dog. . ." His voice drifted before he caught himself. "Everything really. But I guess I had an epiphany, is that the word? This morning. Too many frozen dinners, too much TV. I haven't worked out or gone for a run in almost two years. I need a change."

Matthew bent to lace up his black boots. "I hit the sporting goods store before my shift. Got some running shoes, socks, shorts. I used to run all the time. I'm going to try and get back into that."

Garza's hand grasped his shoulder. "Good for you, brother. You need this. You deserve to get yourself back."

I gotta try, Matthew thought. *One mile at a time.*

The following day, Matthew woke around 2:30 in the afternoon, made a pot of strong coffee, and dressed in his new running gear. He threw an old tank top (*yikes, it's a bit tight!*) and stepped out into the heat of the afternoon. The warm sunlight was like a welcome embrace from an old friend. He hadn't felt the "getting ready to work out" sensation for so long, he feared his body would not cooperate.

13

Fortunately, his fears were unfounded. It took a bit of time for his breathing and pace to match, and he was shockingly winded as he neared his first mile. His commitment to get back in shape, though, outmatched his body. Using the running app on his phone, he already plotted three miles, and whether he ran them or walked them, he didn't care. After Garza's love tap on his belly yesterday, Matthew was even more committed.

Matthew used to have a body that rivaled magazine underwear models. He was certain that was one reason Erica married him in the first place. Attracting women had never been a problem for him; running shirtless in a park would guarantee at least one phone number from an interested potential date.

Today, he felt self-conscious, even wearing the tank top. He knew he faced an uphill battle, but fighting was something he excelled at. Starting as a Marine to his present position as a patrol officer, he fought in some way every day. Tackling this flab would just be another fight he resolved to win.

Mile one ended at the entry to the dirt path that looped around a large nature area and touted a kids' playground, exercise stations along the trail, a pond that park officials called a "lake," and a small dog park. The dog park was where Matthew had often walked with Duggo, and he avoided it for the last several months. Now the pain of his dog's death had lessened, and he barely registered the dog park as he ran past.

Mile two was a horrible run/walk, and Matthew's cheeks flushed with humiliation in addition to exertion. The final mile home loomed long and daunting before him, but he had no choice. How else would he get home? He struggled through the final mile and crashed through his front door. Filling a cup of water from the fridge, he swallowed it in loud, messy gulps. Sweat poured off him in streaming rivulets, stinging his eyes and soaking his clothes. His shirt dripped sweat onto the floor as he dropped his sopping clothes to the bathroom tile and heaved himself into the shower. Shocked that he was gasping from a measly three miles, he allowed the water to spill over him, washing the sweat, grime, and effort of the run down the drain.

Tomorrow will be easier, he told himself, resting his head against the steamy tile.

The next run was *not* easier. In fact, the three miles seemed even more difficult, and Matthew again struggled through the run. The day after was not easier either. In fact, if Matthew were honest with himself, it took nearly two weeks before the three miles began to feel like a work out and not a form of masochism.

He realized quickly that the frozen dinners were not going to help him regain his health or making running easier; they did the opposite. Again, he recognized he must commit completely, so on his next day off he went through the fridge and tossed most of the frozen meals. The labels indicated a few meals were on the healthier side, so he kept those. Then he attacked the pantry, where packages of chips and an old can of spray cheese joined the frozen dinners in the trash.

With an empty fridge and pantry, he perused the local grocery before his run, selecting fruits, salads, chicken, and bottled waters. Now that exercise was becoming his habit, his diet should follow. He also bought an insulated lunch box to bring his healthier food to work instead of finding a greasy burger at 24-hour fast food joint.

Matthew was not certain he would stick with it — the spirit is willing, but the flesh is weak, after all, and he did love his chips — but this was a good start.

Running provided several other benefits for Matthew as well. He lost some of his brain fog, the ruminating cycle of self-pity that enfolded him for the last year. He also noticed he had more energy, and getting in and out of his black-and-white got easier as he finished his third week of running.

A month after his life changes, Garza's snarky tone held a note of appreciation.

"Looking good, Danes. You decided you wanted to get back down to your fighting weight?"

Garza flicked his hand to Matthew's belly again, which may not have shrunk much, but was less rounded than it had been. Matthew's face had started to slim down, and overall, he felt stronger. His chest swelled with pride that someone other than himself noticed.

"Not sure I'll ever see to my Marine weight again, but I'd like to have my woman-magnet look back."

"Well, brother, you are on your way." Garza grabbed his own belly that spilled slightly over his belt buckle. "Maybe I need to start running. I can't imagine that Jazzy is happy with my dad bod."

Matthew mimicked Garza's move from a month ago, patting the man's belly. "Being pregnant is a lot of work, brother," Matthew joked, and Garza jumped back.

"Yeah, I need to get on that. Can't have my woman looking elsewhere." Garza spoke casually and slammed his locker shut, patting Matthew on the shoulder as he left.

Matthew sat in silence, the impact of Garza's words sinking in. Matthew's ex looked elsewhere, and left him when she found someone, but he didn't think he put on the weight until *after* they separated. *Had he?* But Garza and his wife were tight, two kids, new baby on the way, and Jazzy adored Ramon and their family. Matthew shook his head as he watched his beat partner leave.

I think it's more than that, brother. He kept that thought to himself.

Three

Early fall in Southern California is nothing more than an extended late summer — sunny and hot. In fact, his nights on patrol were often busier in September compared to the height of summer in July. The night before was no exception. As Matthew laced up his running shoes for a hot jog in the scorching afternoon sun, he let his mind replay the crazy evening he just worked.

Most nights in So Cal cooled off a little, but the last week had been an oven, both day and night, and the crazies came out with the heat. On those evenings, with sweat dripping under his bulletproof vest and down his back (*the blue polyester uniforms did not breathe for shit*), he went from one call to the next, non-stop movement. Sirens blared throughout night, echoing in the empty streets, and he often had to give chase to a suspect who tried to ditch a weapon or drugs and flee a scene. While he was faster at pursuing a perp, it was a far different exercise to run in a stiff uniform and heavy work boots than in his runners and shorts.

The shift prior, Matthew had sat in his sweltering patrol car. Even at 4 am with the air conditioning on full blast, the heat didn't want to move. He typed into the onboard computer, the glowing screen illuminating the inside of his vehicle. Writing reports would be easier for him if he had paid attention in his high school typing class. Instead, his hunt-and-peck method made for a slow process. He raked his hand through his spiky hair as he finished the final section when his radio chirped to life.

"T44, you copy?" dispatch called to him. Matthew absently pressed the button on his radio.

"This is T44, copy," he said automatically.

"T12 is requesting back up on a domestic. Reporting party claims her boyfriend has a gun."

"Dispatch, T44 enroute." Matthew tossed his clipboard to the passenger seat and put the car in drive as he flipped on his lights and sirens.

The once quiet neighborhood alighted in red and blue, the sirens screeching through the dark streets. He maneuvered the car around and peeled out, racing toward Garza.

Details of the maddening call from the previous shift rolled over his mind as he found his running pace in the park. With all the oppressive heat, drug abusers came out of the woodwork, bath salt users in particular. Since bath salts raise the user's body temp, when that combines with high seasonal temperatures, the end result is cranked, naked, crazed addicts raging in the streets.

Last night, a domestic fight erupted between two people who wore nothing but their birthday suits in the middle of Newport Blvd, blocking traffic and causing a scene. The worse part was when they gave chase — naked users were so sweaty and slick, getting them into custody was a slippery, damp battle. *Much like mud wrestling,* Matthew imagined.

And they had unnatural strength, so several officers needed to pile on to take down each insensible person, and then they had to stand the offenders up as quickly as possible and place them in an air-conditioned car before the druggies' hearts burst from heat and exertion. Officers regularly made trips to the hospital before heading to booking, and the paperwork was astronomical.

Those calls were physically and mentally draining; cops worried during the entire encounter that the drug user would suffer a heart attack in custody and initiate an investigation that, on a cooler day or if the offender abused some other drug, would not happen. Fortunately, last night, no gun was found on either perp, the addicts remained upright, and the booking afterward encountered no glitches.

Matthew recalled the events, evaluating his behavior (wiping his hands on his running shorts in memory of the slimy film that covered the male offender — sometimes the sensation remained even after several showers), checking to make sure he acted by the book. As both offenders were healthy and booked into jail by early morning, Matthew and his brothers in blue considered that a win.

His mind on other matters, he paid little attention as he rounded a sharp curve of the trail. Just as he congratulated himself over a well-executed arrest, a huge German Shepherd ran onto the path, tethered by a long leash. Matthew twisted to the side of the trail to avoid tripping over the dumb beast. The animal emitted one loud bark, and Matthew paused give the dog's owner a dressing down. While he did admire the dog — the animal was a perfect specimen, it could have been a show dog — his mouth, ready to confront the owner, snapped shut.

At the other end of the tethered leash stood a slender, fairly tall woman, bright running shoes extending up to firm, tanned legs. His eyes traveled up her body, over her tiny running shorts that displayed her muscular thighs, over her fitted (*beautifully fitted,* he thought) tank top, to her angular face and sleek, ebony hair pulled back in a tight, low ponytail. Matthew's chest and loins clenched simultaneously, a sensation he had not experienced several years.

The woman reached her hand out to make sure he wasn't going to fall, and Matthew almost took it in his. Shaking his head to clear it, he snatched his hand back.

"You OK?" The woman's liquid voice asked. "Carter just rushed out. He's normally so good and stays by my side, but we haven't gone for a run in several days, and he was excited. I am so sorry."

Concern painted her face. She was rambling, and Matthew bit the inside of his lip to stop a grin.

"No, you are good. I was able to move around him. No blood, no foul."

This time Matthew smiled, and the exotic woman before him returned the gesture in a radiant glow. Matthew fell into that smile and was lost. He didn't even know her name.

"Beautiful dog," he said, trying to keep her engaged.

Her dark eyes sparkled with pride at the poor dog sitting obediently by her side. Carter kept looking down the trail and back at his mistress, probably wondering, *why aren't we running?*

"Oh, thanks," she replied, reaching to give her good boy a pat, and the dog pressed his head against her leg. The dog obviously loved her unconditionally. Matthew just met her and understood the dog's feelings. The electricity he felt from her burned deep within him.

"May I pet him?" Matthew reached forward and placed his hand at the dog's nose when the woman nodded. "Is he a purebred?"

Her silky hair shimmered as she nodded. "Yep, a gift from my parents when I moved out. They didn't want me living by myself."

"Good choice of a dog for that," Matthew told her. "One of my buddies is in the K9 Unit and cannot stop talking about how amazing the dog is. I've seen his shepherd in action more than once, and Germans are so well trained."

"You've seen a K9 in action? Are you a cop?"

Matthew's smile widened. He loved his job, even after asinine nights like the one before, and enjoyed telling people about it.

"Yeah, out of Tustin."

"Oh, do you live near here, then? Not Tustin? Running and all?" She gestured a slender hand at his running shorts. He had a flashing thought he hoped his package looked tempting.

"Yeah, just west of the park." He held out a hand, praying it wasn't too sweaty. He knew from experience how well *that* went over. "I'm Matthew, by the way."

"Oh, I'm Rosemarie." She grasped his hand in a surprisingly firm grip. He wanted to let her fingers linger in his but was afraid it would come off as creepy.

"And this is Carter?" He squatted and rubbed the dog's head affectionately. Rosemarie crouched next to him, beaming at her dog.

"Yeah. We normally run this trail earlier in the day, before work, but I've been sick, and so this is the first day in over a week I made it out here."

"Well, he looks happy to finally be out here with you." Matthew gave the dog another quick pet, then stood. "I would love to stay here and chat with you more, but I think Carter would lose patience."

Matthew let the suggestion hang in the air, gearing up some courage to ask for her number. Rosemarie solved that dilemma for him.

"Why don't I get your number?" she asked. "And maybe we can meet up for a run with you."

Matthew's heart was full to bursting. While it wasn't as great as getting her number, the fact she took the first step was a good start. As he read out his numbers for her to put in her phone, he thanked all the higher powers he could think of that he started his diet and running over a month earlier, so he was in better shape for this meeting. Would she have chatted him up if he were still pudgier? Who knew? She may not care, but *he* did. Rosemarie looked up at him as she finished thumb-typing.

"Here, let's make sure I got it right."

She pressed her phone screen, and his phone dinged in his pocket. Matthew nearly fainted. He didn't have to ask for her phone number; she sent it right to him, no questions asked. His lucky, lucky day, the first one in a long while. Glancing at his phone, he thumbed open the "add to contact" window to save the number.

"Yep, we are good." Matthew raised his eyes to hers, once again losing himself. "It was great to meet you, Rosemarie, and Carter, too. Feel free to call or text me anytime."

There, the offer was out in the open. Rosemarie's toothy smile widened.

"Oh, I will."

Matthew's feet barely touched the ground for the rest of his run. He had the idea that Rosemarie watched him as he ran off, and he hoped his ass looked good in the tight running shorts. His sorry excuse for a tank top could not be helped, so he shrugged it off. Checking his running app when he walked through his front door, he laughed as he noted his fastest running time yet, not counting the chat with Rosemarie and her dog. With buoyed spirits, Matthew jumped in the shower and headed out to work, silky black hair and sparkling dark eyes occupying his mind.

His preoccupation was not lost on Garza. The man missed nothing.

"Hey, brother. What's making you so happy today? Or is it a who?" Ramon waggled his eyebrows suggestively.

"Haha, Garza." Matthew whacked him on the arm.

"No, brother, really. You are fucking shining!"

Matthew ducked his head, trying to hide the blush that stained his cheeks. He felt like a kid again. And after being stuck for so long in his dark place under his rock of sadness, a ray of happiness radiated from him like the heat off the sidewalk on an August afternoon.

"Bro, I met someone."

"No shit." Garza's eyes comically popped out of their sockets. That was the last thing Garza expected to hear. "Who is she?"

"Well, I mean I just met her. Today. This afternoon, on my run. I tripped over her dog."

"Whoa, and she has a dog. Big step for you, man."

"Yeah, but she took my number."

Garza rolled his eyes, indicating what he thought of that move. Matthew shook his head and grinned with one side of his mouth.

"And then she texted me right away, so I have hers." Matthew pulled her info up on his phone and waved it in Garza's face.

"Holy shit! She got your number and then texted you? Did you pay her or something?"

"What? Hell, no, Garza."

Ramon looked Matthew up and down, approvingly.

"You have gotten in a bit of shape, and your overall personality has improved, so maybe she is interested. You gonna call her?"

"Text her, maybe. I dunno. I'll probably wait till tomorrow or Sunday. I don't want to look over eager or creepy or anything."

"Brother, you can't help but look creepy," Garza told him and bobbed away as Matthew feigned a punch in his direction.

Four

That night, another hot night full of insanity, he held over so he didn't get home until almost noon and slept through his normal run. Around 6 pm, his phone pinged a text message, and he awoke with crusty eyes trying to focus into a bleary room. *Who's texting me?* Peering at his phone with the one eye he managed to pry open, he made out the blurry name. *Rosemarie.* What the hell? She was texting him already? Who did that? Who was this woman?

Hey there Matthew. I just wanted to see if you were running tomorrow. Carter and I would enjoy a lap around the park!

Did he get asked out on a date? A running date? *What was going on here?* If anyone told him a month ago that he would be asked out on a running date with a hot young woman, he would have laughed in their face, probably spitting chip crumbs out in the process.

Not wanting to look too eager, he set his phone to the side and collapsed back into his pillows, rubbing the grit out of his eyes. After years out of the dating scene, including having to chase Erica just to date him in the first place, having a woman come on to him this hard (at least it seemed hard to him) was a welcome change. Most likely what he needed, otherwise he would not have nabbed her number, let alone a date.

A date? Did this count as a date? Was he reading too much into a simple run?

A run *tomorrow*? Disoriented, he flipped his phone to up see what day it was. Sunday. His first day off, and he slept through it. Overtime always knocked him out hard — always had. Some brothers in blue, could work a 17-hour shift, sleep for three hours, and be ready to for their next shift. The night shift, while it was Matthew's preferred time slot, meant his circadian rhythm was already out of whack. Overtime wiped him out, and he slept like a toddler.

Having slept hard today, he wanted to enjoy the rest of his day off, so instead of running, cleaning, or laundry – his typical first day off list of duties – he dragged his lagging ass out of bed and hopped in the shower.

After the past month of great eating, a fine Sunday night meal — a steak dinner, salad, no potatoes — sounded like a treat. The local steakhouse was nearly empty, and afterward he returned to the sporting goods store. If he were going to run with Rosemarie tomorrow, he wanted something nicer than his ratty (*now better fitting, thank*

GOD) tank top and the one pair of running shorts he owned.

The cashier rang up a stylish running shirt, a new pair of running shorts, and a fresh pair of socks. Satisfied he wouldn't show up looking frumpy, he smiled to himself as sat in his car with his new purchases, sending a text back to Rosemarie.

Sorry for the late response. I worked overtime and slept most of today. Running with you tomorrow sounds great. Keeping me honest! What time do you want to meet at the park?

Matthew hit the send button before he could reread or rethink his message, and hoping he didn't sound too eager, waited for a reply. His phone dinged a text notification after a few seconds. Matthew's smile broadened, giddiness bubbling inside him.

Do you prefer a morning or afternoon run?

Matthew had to think. If they ran in the morning, there was a chance he could ask her out for a date later that night. Then a thought hit him — tomorrow was Monday. Did she have to work? Her text made it sound as though she had the day off. Did she have that kind of flexible job? And if they did a morning run, and she was still as amazing as she appeared so far, should he ask her out on a date that evening? Was there any protocol on that? His heart raced at the thought, and small butterflies, more like moths really, fluttered in his stomach as he texted her back.

I can do either. Why don't we try for the morning?

His phone dinged back her response: *Want to get it over with early, huh?*

His grin was uncontrollable. If only she knew the truth.

Better to not delay the agony of a run! LOL.

Does 9 am sound ok?

Could he wait until 9 am to see her? When did he start acting like a smitten middle-schooler?

9 am sounds great. See you then!

Five

Monday morning blazed bright and hot, but not nearly as bright or hot as Rosemarie. She was like a dark sun as she sauntered up to Matthew who waited near the dog park. Carter lopped at her side, excited and ready for his run. Matthew squatted to welcome the happy dog. After patting the him and rubbing his ears, Matthew stood, smiling at Rosemarie. She returned the smile, a beacon against her dusky skin, and his heart skipped a beat again.

"I'm glad you wanted to go for a run," she told him. "I usually only run with Carter, but he seemed to like you well enough, and since we interrupted your run the other day, I thought it would be a good way to make it up to you."

"You don't need to make up for anything," he replied, hoping his voice did not sound as sappy to her as it did to him. "But I am glad you texted. I don't normally have a running partner at all, unlike you." He gestured to the dog.

"Yeah, he's a great runner," she explained, "but he sucks at small talk."

Her grin widened, softening the sharp, exquisite angle of her face, and if her personality was even half as attractive, he was doomed. Matthew was already smitten by her light banter.

"I only started back a month or so ago after a long hiatus, so if I'm too slow, feel free to take off. I'll catch up when you're done."

"Well, Carter can get a great clip going, but I can be a slower runner, so you go ahead and set the pace."

She looped Carter's leash around a band on her waist, and the dog took the lead, Matthew and Rosemarie falling into step behind him.

The initial conversation was about as impressive as talking about the weather, but as Matthew learned more about her, he found her more intriguing. She owned a small wine bar on the far east side of town, almost on the Santa Ana/Tustin town border. Mondays and Tuesdays were her days off — she actually closed the bar on those days.

"No business at all. No one needs wine until hump day, so Wednesdays are super busy," she said with a gentle laugh.

Matthew considered it serendipitous that she had the same days off as he did. And she worked close to his patrol area? What were the odds? He sent another silent *thank you* up to the universe.

The conversation turned to her dog, and as they chatted, panting a bit at the pace, he surprised himself by opening up and telling her about Duggo.

"Oh, I am so sorry, Matthew."

She stopped her run to face him. Carter looked up at his mistress and whined in confusion. She placed her hand on Matthew's arm in consolation, a tingling racing up to his chest from her light touch.

"I would be absolutely distraught if anything happened to Carter."

"It's OK. It's been almost two years. It still hurts a bit, but more like a scar than a giant bruise. Thank you for that though."

His voice was heavy as he patted her hand, delighted at their continued focus on each other. Rosemarie's eyes softened at him, and she squeezed his arm briefly before pulling her hand away. The emotion swooned over him about his dog, not his ex, which surprised him. With a passing thought, he considered when he should broach *that* subject. Was there a procedure on discussing one's divorce?

Rosemarie checked their distance on her phone. "We are almost at three miles. Do you want to finish the loop around the playground and call it a run?"

No, he thought, panicked, *I don't want it to end.* Instead, he replied, "That sounds good. Do —" and he paused.

Rosemarie flipped her eyes to his. "You were saying?"

Matthew glanced his eyes down at the ground, gathering his courage, then caught Rosemarie's ebony gaze with his own azure one. He wondered if she felt the same dark and bright chemistry he did.

"I know a coffee place down the road. They have an outdoor area and people bring their dogs all the time. Would you want to grab a coffee or something? We would even finish the run there."

She didn't even check the time, responding immediately. "That's a great idea!" She sounded truly excited at the prospect.

"I would offer to race you, but I think you would beat me."

"I suck at racing," she said. "And the dog would beat us both anyway," she joked as she took off, leaving Matthew to catch up.

Sweat poured off Matthew's forehead as he walked into the welcome air-conditioned interior of the coffee shop. Rosemarie, who looked like she just stepped out of the house and not like she completed a three-mile run, perched on a deck chair outside with Carter, having given Matthew her order when he asked.   He turned down the cash she offered, *like a true gentleman,* he thought. What kind of person would he be if he didn't pay for her freaking cup of coffee?

He occupied himself on his phone as he waited for the server to call his name. Garza had texted him about some of the calls they had worked earlier in the week and bitched a bit about the new baby's lack of napping. Garza took a week off when the baby was born but was already back and looking like a sleep-weary new dad. He also was not the type who could work on only three hours of sleep.

Matthew chuckled inwardly and peered out the window, watching Rosemarie scratch at Carter, who lay at her feet in blissful oblivion. She scrolled through her phone with her other hand, her finger working in a mesmerizing cadence. He shook his head to clear it and gave a nervous sigh. *Don't screw this up, man,* he admonished himself.

Grabbing the coffees when the barista finally called him, Matthew had also bought a bottle of water, for either Rosemarie or the dog, whoever needed it more. He juggled the drinks as he stepped out the door, and Rosemarie jumped up to help him.

"Thanks so much. This was a nice idea. Today is a beautiful day."

They sat at the table, the dark brown umbrella covering them in a dappled shade. Matthew popped open the water and waved it toward the dog reclining under the table.

"May I?" he asked. Rosemarie swallowed her sip of macchiato.

"Of course. Thank you. My bottled water was nearly empty and warm, poor dog."

Matthew poured it in the dog's mouth, enjoying how the dog lapped at the rush of water. Carter didn't lift his head off the ground as he drank, letting Matthew do all the work.

"Lazy dog," Rosemarie lamented, and Matthew grinned at her.

She sighed at his dimples that played peek-a-boo on his smiling cheeks. Did he have any idea how cute he was? To Rosemarie, he was like a shiny coin, golden, bright, and sparkly. His blue eyes danced as he told her about his work, his strong hands working the steaming paper cup of coffee.

"So, are you thinking about getting a dog? Or is it still too raw?" Rosemarie ventured.

Matthew shrugged. "I don't know yet. I don't think I can get the same breed of dog, but Duggo was a mutt, so getting the same type would be hard. I'm getting there, though."

"That's good. I never had a dog until Carter. This is a whole new thing for me. He makes me less lonely though, so that is good."

The word "lonely" hung in the air like thick smoke. Rosemarie was adventurous with her language, with her actions. Was this her way of letting him know he could show his more vulnerable side? Was she encouraging him to be bold, adventurous? Matthew forced himself to gaze into the dark pools of her eyes.

"I can't imagine someone as beautiful as you lonely," he told her. A gentle blush stained Rosemarie's cheek, deepening her tanned skin. Matthew bit back a smile but kept his electric gaze steady.

"Well, I know they say not to talk about exes on a first date, but are you OK if I tell you?"

"I guess it depends on what you tell me, but yes."

It was his attempt to make light of the conversation. And he did want to hear about how someone so lovely could be single. Single and interested in *him*.

"I dated a guy for a while. We even talked about moving in together." A wry smirk tugged at her lips. "But he kept drinking more than I liked, always wanting to go to the bar, and that's not me. I *work* in a bar! I wanted trips to the beach, to the mountains, to museums. To get out and have fun, not sit in a dark bar. And we started fighting. Carter did not like his fighting with me, and I took my cue from the dog. They are great judges of character, after all."

Matthew glanced down at the dog, who resembled a passed-out drunk under the full shade of the patio table. He was like a German Shepherd rug.

"I understand that. Dogs can tell you a lot about a person."

"What about you?" Rosemarie pried. "What's a nice guy like you doing single?"

Matthew cringed at the "nice" reference. *Please don't let her want to just be friends,* he hoped before answering.

"Maybe not so nice. Since I'm a cop, I have to have that stern demeanor. I work late, overtime, mostly night shift, which is not the best schedule. I was married for several years, but she didn't like the schedule, didn't like how I sometimes needed to decompress after a bad night, and maybe I didn't give her enough attention. She looked for it somewhere else. That was more than two years ago."

"So, you've been single for a while? My break up was less than a year ago, and I took my time getting back in the game."

He chuckled at her phrasing. Tough language for such a feminine woman. "I dated off and on, but my heart wasn't in it. I think I lost myself for a while. I have spent the last few months trying to get myself back on track."

"And the running?" Rosemarie wagged her hand down Matthew's frame. "Is that helping you get back on track?"

"To say the least. That was to get rid of some excess weight. I'm also a former Marine. I was *not* happy with extra flab. I knew it wasn't healthy."

Something about what he said struck Rosemarie as hilarious, and she laughed wildly, her teeth bright, her hair waving, her breasts heaving.

"What's so funny?" he asked, wanting to laugh with her.

"Isn't that why we all run? To get rid of that weight?" She could barely speak, trying to catch her breath after laughing. "I was pudgy in high school. I started running to lose some of the weight. That and swimming. Now I use it to keep it off, and it became a habit." She paused. "It was funny because I think that's the only reason people run. I mean, who does this because they actually like it?"

38

Matthew found himself laughing along with her, her onyx eyes dancing with delight. He didn't want the date to end. *Fortune favors the bold*, he told himself.

"When can I see you again?" he asked suddenly. He reached across the short span of the table and touched his broad finger to her dainty one. She did not pull away.

Rosemarie's laugh died down, and he was lost in her dark, sparkling gaze. Her lips pulled into a slanted smile.

"What?" she teased. "We just spent the morning running, then came for coffee. It's already after noon!"

"Tonight?" That one word drew her attention; his blue gaze never left her face. Rosemarie looked confused.

"But we spent the morning together. Why would you want a date for tonight?"

I want a date with you every day and night, he thought, his lips curving deeply, making his dimples dance. He put it all out on the table.

"I find you an amazing woman, Rosemarie. Everything about you intrigues me, and then you have this earnestness, this honesty I have not seen from anyone in a long, long time. And you are strikingly beautiful on top of all that. The more time I spend with you, the more I want to spend time with you. Does that make any sense?"

The dusky blush returned to her cheeks, and she cast her eyes down to Carter, who still lolled about in happy exhaustion under the table.

"Well, flattery will only get you so far." She paused and looked past him toward the busy street. Contemplation shrouded her face.

"What were you thinking for tonight?" she asked.

Matthew's face lit up like a Christmas tree, full of color and joy. "Normally I'd say something like a wine bar," he wagged his eyebrows at her. "But since you own a wine bar, let's try a different atmosphere. Are you up for an Irish pub? There is a place called the Claddagh Ring, right off downtown. On the weekends they have loud Irish bands, but tonight would be quiet. Does that sound good?"

Matthew held his breath, as though his whole life depended on her answer.

"I don't usually have the bar open on Monday nights, so I'm not busy. An Irish pub sounds fun. I'll go."

Matthew had to restrain himself from jumping up in euphoria. Instead, his smile was huge, fit to split his face.

"Can it be an official date? Can I pick you up at your house?"

Rosemarie tipped her head to the side. The handsome blond cop in front of her seemed worth the chance. She nodded.

"Yeah, I'll text you my address." She glanced at her phone. "But I have a few things to do, not the least of which is shower and get ready for this big date I have tonight. What time should I expect you?"

Matthew glanced at his watch. It was already after one.

"How about six? I'll make a reservation for 6:30, just in case?"

When Rosemarie answered the door, Matthew's heart caught in his throat. She was striking in her every day running gear, but dressed for a night out, in a slick, black body suit and her shimmery dark hair bound on one side, she remined him of a model stepping off the cover of a magazine. He managed to find his voice and held out his arm to her.

"Shall we?" Trying to sound nonchalant, he had to work to keep his arm from shaking when she grasped it and graced him with a brilliant smile. His insides melted. If she were nervous, she hid it well.

The usually loud Irish bar scene was subdued for the Monday night crowd. The darkened stage sat silent at the far end of the bar, and plenty of tables clustered around a central bar. Coats of arms and plaid tartan art on the walls created a wonderfully pseudo-Irish environment. Rosemarie had never been inside this pub, even though it was not far from her own wine bar. She assumed Matthew was familiar with the pub because it was in the city of Tustin proper, and she asked if he worked nearby.

"Yep, it's part of my patrol area. I patrol the whole west side."

"More than just you?" she asked as the hostess showed them to their table. "Do you have a partner or something?"

"I have beat partners, other brothers in blue assigned the same patrol area. We go to other areas as needed, but we mostly drive around our patrol area."

Rosemarie's face glowed in the darkened restaurant. "Brothers in blue. I like that. Very cop-like."

Matthew laughed at her comment, his broad chest quaking under his dark gray button down. "Like I'm really a cop?"

She tilted her head, giddy over the light banter. "Yeah, you don't seem like a cop."

His wavy, golden hair and bright eyes were attractively set off by his dress shirt. Matthew looked like a college student, not a police officer.

"But you could pull me over anytime," she flirted.

Matthew's eyes fixated on her, sparkling with intensity. His blue gaze was a laser that cut deep, and her heart raced as he studied her. He leaned forward, electricity popping between them.

"I'll have to remember that," he responded, his voice husky.

Then the waitress arrived at their table, and he sat up, clearing his throat. They both grabbed their menus, blushing.

"Do you want an appetizer?" Matthew offered.

They put in their appetizer, drink, and dinner orders, and once the waitress left, they again leaned into the table toward each other. Matthew brazenly reached across the table, taking her hand in his. He ran his thumb over her dainty fingers.

"How did you decide to become a cop?" Rosemarie asked. It had been a while since she felt interested in anyone, but Matthew had a magnetic pull on her, and she wanted to know more about him.

"I was in the military, a Marine, for a few years, and when I got out, policing was a way to still have that type of job, but not have to travel. Since I was getting married, I didn't want to travel that much. I've been with Tustin for almost ten years."

"So, running is a familiar workout for you," Rosemarie surmised, "military and all."

Matthew nodded.

"I fell out of shape for a bit, so going back to my military roots is how I got back into it."

"Too many donuts?" she joked. Matthew chuckled good naturedly.

"Ha ha. Too many cop TV shows with that one!" He dipped his head, acknowledging the stereotype. "But I don't like donuts," he confessed. "What about you? Owning a wine bar is not a job you hear about every day."

Rosemarie finished her bite of cheese stick and washed it down with a sip of her Irish cream before answering.

"It's not fully my bar, to be honest."

Matthew threw up a hand in mock indignation. "Scandalous!"

Rosemarie beamed. "My best friend from college, her family owns one of those large wineries in Napa. I had my business degree but no job to go with it. I wanted to open a restaurant or something, and my friend asked her parents if they could help get it up and running. They helped so much, and they are essentially my 'silent partner.' It's mostly my bar. I run it and make all the decisions, but I get most of my supplies and wine for cheap from them. If you come into the bar sometime, you'll see that Jensen wines are the featured wine. Just about everything says Jensen on it inside the bar!" Rosemarie giggled.

Matthew could not help but notice how she glowed when she talked about her bar.

"Is that an invitation? Could I stop by the bar sometime?" Matthew asked, his face open and earnest. Rosemarie stopped giggling, her insides at once both hot and fluttering.

"Only if I get to see you in your uniform," she countered. Matthew's face lit up.

"I can arrange that. If you want, we can go to my house after dinner and I'll model it for you."

Rosemarie's eyebrows arose alarmingly, and realization dawned on Matthew's face.

"Oh no! I didn't mean —! I was just saying —" he sputtered, and Rosemarie could not help but smirk at his discomfort. She reached over and touched his chin with a slender finger, pulling his gaze up to meet hers.

"Are you saying you don't want me to come by your place tonight?"

Her eyes held a suggestive promise. His own intensity returned.

"The opposite," he breathed. "I would like for you to come over, very much." He placed his hand over hers, keeping it on his face. "Would you want to come by?"

Before she could answer, the waitress came by with their dinners, and Matthew cursed her timing.

Six

They continued to make small talk as they ate, the heat of the earlier conversation having dissipated with the arrival of their meal. The attraction between them, however, remained, an electric magnetism that buzzed about their table. The more time they spent together, the more powerful that electricity seemed to become. Matthew's insides were on fire, Rosemarie's mere presence burning him from the inside out. He only hoped her insides burned like that for him. From the tone of her comments, he thought maybe she did.

He finished his fish and chips (he wanted to clean meal, as to not drip anything on his shirt. He didn't want to imagine what impression *that* would make) and waited politely as Rosemarie to finish her dinner. She left some on her plate but turned down the waitress's offer for a take-home box.

"I'm not going home right now," she told the waitress while keeping her eyesight on Matthew. His dick throbbed with excitement at her suggestion, and he was grateful they would have to wait for the bill and he didn't have to stand up. *That* was another impression he did not want to leave with her.

Matthew paid the bill when it arrived, and they left the pub for Matthew's house. He kept his eyes on her as he opened his front door, gauging her reaction. Fortunately, he had the presence of mind to tidy up the house the day before, and the kitchen and hall bathroom were wiped down. While he didn't think she would come to his house that evening, he liked to be prepared. The last thing he wanted was for Rosemarie to think he was a slob of a bachelor.

She did a pretty thorough once-over, then smiled over her shoulder at him, her dark hair swinging.

"Nice house. Bigger than I thought."

"Well, that's a perk," he tried to joke.

"I guess I'm used to the slummy apartment bachelor pads. This is a surprise."

"Thank you," he said, reclining against the entryway.

"Right now, it's probably cleaner than my house," she said, and his eyebrows flew up in disbelief.

Her mouth curved upwards. She enjoyed keeping him on his toes. She dropped her purse next to the couch and sat down.

"Well?" she questioned, her delicate, oval face upturned.

Matthew's eyes crinkled in confusion. "Well, what?"

"Your uniform?" Her curved lips parted further.

His entire body leapt off the door frame. "Oh, you were serious?"

"As a heart attack. Other than getting pulled over for speeding once, I've never been near an officer in full uniform. I want to cross that off my bucket list."

He returned Rosemarie's smile and stepped toward the hall. "I'll be right back, then."

As he left into the recesses of the hallway, Rosemarie let her eyes scan around his family room. The non-descript micro-fiber couch naturally faced the large flat-screen TV, a selection of video game paraphernalia tucked next to it on a short bookcase. A colorful piece of abstract art hung on the wall that led to the hall, and the shiny, dark coffee table hosted a stack of coasters and a video game controller.

Coasters? She thought. A strange item in a bachelor's house. Perhaps a holdover from his ex?

A rustling noise attracted her attention and she looked up, her breath catching in her chest.

When you get pulled over by cops, their navy-blue uniforms and flashing lights cause fear and stress. But when you are on a date with the cop, and he puts on his uniform for the fun of it for you, a whole new onslaught of emotions accompany that vision.

Matthew was tall and broad-shouldered to begin with. His uniform with the vest underneath, gun belt on his hip, only emphasized the powerful presentation of his body, exuding masculinity and virility. Rosemarie's heart quickened, the familiar pulling sensation between her legs distracting her almost as much as the presence of Matthew in full police uniform.

He stood awkwardly in the middle of the living room, his thumbs hooked into this belt, letting her eyes roam over him. She stood in one eloquent move, reaching out to run her fingers along the edges of his badge, the seams of his shirt, the line of his belt. His muscles were rock hard beneath her touch, and his cock flexed in automatic response. The quiet of the room was accentuated only by the sound of her fingers slipping over the fabric and their shared, heavy breathing.

Rosemarie traced the etched name tag affixed to his solid chest, tapping it with a long fingernail.

"Officer Danes?" she asked, one eyebrow raised in an enticing invitation. Matthew dipped his head.

"Ma'am," he said in a commanding voice.

She allowed her fingers to continue over his stiff uniform. She tapped the handcuffs, and the clinking sound broke the silence. She bit her lip as a leisurely smile spread across her flushed cheeks.

"Should I take them out?" he asked, his strong voice husky. His blood pounded through his chest, and he struggled to control his thoughts.

"Yes."

With a deft move, he plucked the handcuffs off the belt. The cuffs dangled before her shining eyes for a moment, then he gently grasped her hand and captured her wrist in the metal restraints. She wiggled her hand, the cuffs jingling.

"Heavier than I thought they would be," she told him.

She held up her wrist, and he stood there staring stupidly at her hand.

"Well?" she asked again. Matthew's brow furrowed. "Aren't you going to arrest me?" she continued, her voice husky.

Matthew leaned in close to her, clasping her other hand in his strong fingers and spun her around, trapping her wrists behind her back. He snapped the second cuff into place, and her sleek form was at his mercy. He leaned in even more, placing his lips close to the exposed side of her neck where her hair pulled to the side. His breath tickled the little hairs on her neck and warmed her skin, and she shivered in response.

When she cleared her throat to regain her senses, Matthew caught the hint and removed the handcuffs in one smooth movement, her hands once again free.

Matthew reached behind himself to replace the cuffs, then lifted her palm to his lips. He trailed his mouth over the length of her sensitive, trembling wrist, and her knees grew weak. They caught each other's eyes, dark on bright. Her black eyes reflected the dim light in the room, shining like dark stars, and he could not stop his own arms from wrapping around her slim waist. She stretched up on

49

her strong runner's legs and pushed her mouth against Matthew's. He returned the kiss like a starving man consumes food — ravenously, forcefully, with wild abandon.

They clung to each other, gasping and breathless, kissing and licking as though they would never get enough. Rosemarie's lips became more aggressive, her tongue more assertive, sliding between his lips to play against his tongue. Matthew was powerless to stop the long moan that drew from his throat, and Rosemarie nestled closer to him in response.

She clutched his vest through his shirt, trying to pull Matthew even closer, and his hands dropped to her rear, molding the round mounds of her ass in his grasp. They worked their way to the couch, Matthew pulling Rosemarie atop him. He worked his hands on her hips and ass, relishing the sensation of her lips on his mouth, his jaw, and moving down his neck. Her dainty fingers found a shocking strength and seized his hair, clutching at him.

His erection pulsed with each thrust of her mouth and tongue, and she reached her hand down, enveloping his length over his uniform pants. His cock throbbed achingly in her grip. Rosemarie flexed her fingers in response, and he groaned again.

Rosemarie suddenly thrust upward, pushing herself halfway off Matthew's lap, her face flushed and bemused all at once.

"I think I need to stop here," she whispered breathless. "I don't want you to think I'm the type of girl who fucks on the first date."

"It's not," Matthew managed to choke out, his voice labored and raspy.

"What?"

"It's not," he repeated, clearing his throat and adjusting his position on the couch. "This is our third date. Socially acceptable, if you wanted to get busy." He raised his hand in sudden protest, his wide eyes expressing shock at his own forward statement. "Not that I'm trying to pressure you! I'm just saying your count is off."

Her laugh was low, throaty, and she pressed her palm against his upraised hand, lacing her fingers through his.

"No pressure, Officer Danes," she said lightly. "But how do you get three dates?"

"Oh," he touched her fingertips against his lips, kissing a fingertip at each mention. "Date one, our run this morning. Date two, the coffeehouse. Date three, the pub."

Rosemarie's face broke in amused awareness. "You counted all of those as separate dates?"

"Oh my God, Rosemarie, do you have any idea how nervous I was to ask you out for coffee, let alone dinner? The stress of those each constitutes a date. And you asked me out for our first running date."

"Well, that does make a difference." She leaned forward and worked his lips with hers briefly, then sat up on him again. "But I need to give you a reason to ask me out again. So, I think I have to head home."

"Yes, sweetheart," Matthew responded without pause. He wiggled his way out from under her legs to stand and held his hand out in a gallant gesture.

"Let me escort you home then."

"Will you wear your uniform? How sexy would that be to get an honest-to-God police escort?"

Matthew couldn't control the laughter that burst from him. "Of course. Your chariot awaits, milady," he responded as he held her hand, walking her back out to his car.

He walked on clouds, but his heart was heavy. He didn't want her to leave, sex or not. Rosemarie's presence with him helped him feel empowered, full of life, and excited about the future for the first time in years.

Seven

Incapable of focusing on anything else, Matthew spent the next week with Rosemarie on his mind. While his job kept him busy enough to get him through the week, images and thoughts of Rosemarie consumed every free moment otherwise. Her sleek black hair and eyes, her dusky skin, her strong legs and arms, her forceful kissing — Matthew wanted more, so much more, but worried he could chase her away if he showed how enraptured he was or pursued her too hard.

They met up to run twice that week, Rosemarie passionately kissing him hello and goodbye each time. After the second run, covered in sweat and grime, he again decided to be bold.

"Could I come by sometime, maybe before my shift starts, and see you at your wine bar?"

Her infectious smile derailed him; he almost forgot his own question. "I would like to show you my bar," she gushed, her face brightening at his suggestion. She drew back, her hand on her beautiful chest. "Oh, was that too eager? I just speak my mind, and a lot of times, there is no filter."

His open expression told her as much as his words did.

"Hell no! I was worried that I was being too eager! I'm glad to know it's not just me!"

Rosemarie's smile faltered slightly as she trembled at his words. "Alright, we are OK, both being too eager? I don't want you to think I want to push you or rush into anything."

Matthew stared at her, mouth agape, then burst into a fit of laughter. "Oh babe, I haven't dated seriously in the last two years. The last thing I would say is I'm rushing into anything!"

His dimples peeked in and out, and she grew lightheaded at his nearness. Her eyes clouded as she grasped his hands and stepped close to him, inhaling his heady, post-run scent.

"I'm sorry it took you so long to find yourself eager for someone." The intensity in her eyes penetrated him, and he pulled her even tighter to him.

"I would have waited forever for you," he admitted to her.

He blushed at his own words, but his gaze never faltered. Rosemarie clasped his face between her hands and kissed him gently, working his lips. Matthew dropped his hands to wrap her in his strong embrace, then pulled away to catch her face in his calloused hands.

"Are you ok with a visit?" he asked, returning to his original question.

"Will you come in uniform?"

"I can," he answered without hesitation.

"I would love to show off my cop," she said in her silky voice.

His heart jumped into his throat at her words, "my cop." He had to clear his throat to speak again.

"When would be good? Probably not tonight or Saturday. How about Sunday evening? I'm working overtime. Or is that too busy?"

"No, it's perfect, nice and subdued. About what time can I expect you?"

A light breeze caught her hair in a silken flair, and she brushed the ebony tendrils off her face in an unconscious gesture. Matthew shook his head to refocus on her question.

"My shift starts at 8, so if I get there between 6:30 and 7, I can hang out for a while, but not take up too much time."

Rosemarie leaned close to kiss him again. "You can take up as much time as you like."

Matthew spent his weekend alone, running errands, playing video games, and trying to keep up his healthy eating. Video games did not help, as gaming lent itself to chips and snacks, but he compromised with some veggies and blue cheese dip. He read a few social media messages from Garza, most of which were graphic videos and suggestive comments about how Matthew had spent his time over the past week. Matthew commented back with his own bawdy jokes but did not correct Garza's assumptions.

He called his mom, took his car in for detailing, and attacked the bedroom which was truly in desperate need of a cleaning. In retrospect, he was relieved that Rosemarie did not want to go any further Monday night — his sheets were not ready for any action.

Over the entire weekend, his thoughts continued to float back to Rosemarie, the sound of her laugh, the feel of her hot skin on his hands, and he cursed himself. It had been so long since he was enamored by someone.

If he were honest with himself, he could not recall feeling this infatuated with Erica; he certainly didn't feel this way for any of his casual dates after her. Maybe he needed all that time alone to get right in his head and his heart. Regardless, Rosemarie captivated him in a way he had never felt before. His tough cop exterior may not show it, but he became a smitten puppy whenever he was with her.

As much as he hated to admit it, he had fallen hard for his outgoing running partner. The idea of love at first sight was a joke, a cliché, he knew, but perhaps two or three dates? A meeting of the minds and the heart? The heat between them reflected like a sensuous light, illuminating them in a passionate moonlight dance, one that he did not want to end. A moment as simple as talking over coffee, her voice calm and soothing, buoyed his spirits so that dealing with the worst the world had to offer while he was in uniform could not drag him down.

And knowing he would see her again on Sunday night, in her own element, an independent woman in her own right who didn't need him but wanted him?

Maybe not love at first sight, but definitely love at second sight. Matthew had fallen madly and fiercely in love with his raven-haired, dog-loving beauty.

Eight

The florist halfway down Warner Avenue was getting ready to close up shop when Matthew raced in for flowers. A large bouquet of roses and a fun wine card with the message, *I love every moment with you,* earned a wink from the graying cashier. Either that or the uniform — some people, especially business owners, loved it when cops shopped in uniform. The card was another risk. The fear of rushing in or pushing her too hard continually needled at the back of his mind. It seemed each time Matthew turned around, he risked exposing his heart to her, but he couldn't help himself. While it wasn't exactly what he wanted to say, it still conveyed his emotions.

An illuminated wine glass sign greeted him just after 6:30, the scroll-worked *Wine Time* blazing against the darkening sky. He parked in the lot behind the building and tried to appear casual as he entered the frosted-glass front doors.

Deep wood tones and more frosted glass welcomed him at the entrance area of the bar. Amusing wine decor adorned the walls, hints of flax and burgundy adding a touch of color. Wine glasses and bottles shimmered everywhere — on shelves, on the counters, even on the hostess station set back from the door. The perky blonde hostess smiled widely when she saw him step over, the rose bouquet clenched in his hand.

"Hi, can I help you?"

"Yeah, is Rosemarie here?"

"Uh-huh. Miss Lee is in the back. I'll take you to the bar and go get her."

She waved her fingers to have Matthew follow as the blonde wound her way to the bar. Rosemarie was not wrong; the prominent wine bottles and glasses all had "Jensen" emblazoned in gold on them. Several couples huddled together at a plush booth, ignoring him in their romantic interlude. A few young men in crumpled hats sat at the end of the bar counter while a small group of women celebrated some special event at one of the three larger tables. Matthew smiled to himself as he took in the atmosphere This was a wine bar to be proud of.

"Hello, Officer Danes," Rosemarie's sexy voice called from behind him.

He rotated and watched her step around the bar, a vision in her starched white shirt that drew attention to her the dramatic silkiness of her hair and eyes. She wiped her

59

hands on the folded black apron tied around her waist before she reached for him.

"Is it OK for me to kiss you in public? When you are wearing your uniform, I mean? That doesn't break some cop rule, does it?"

"No, I think we are ok. As long as I didn't bend you over my cop car," he responded in a joking tone, and Rosemarie's laugh was contagious.

She fanned herself as she got control of her laughter, then leaned over to kiss him full on the lips, her fingertips lingering on his chest.

"Well, what do you think?" she asked, swirling her hands around at the bar. He nodded in approval.

"This is really nice. I wasn't sure what to expect, not having been to many wine bars, but this is nicer than I could have imagined." He pointed to the sparkling glass throughout the bar. "And you were not joking. The Jensen name is everywhere."

"This wouldn't have happened without them, and they have nice stuff, so I am more than OK with it."

"I like all the grape decor up front."

"I tried for a slightly quirky look throughout. I think it's fun." Her chest swelled as she spoke. The pride in her voice was unmistakable.

"I could not agree more," he concurred with a kiss on her cheek.

Rosemarie slid behind the bar and pulled down a stemless Jensen glass. "I would offer you wine, but I can't imagine you would drink before work?"

"Yeah, being drunk on the job would not go over well with my sergeant."

"How about a water or soda? I have regular, diet, lemon-lime . . ." She gestured to the bar.

"I'll take a diet soda," he said.

Their time together passed too quickly for him. He checked his watch, and 7:25 flashed annoyingly. Matthew's blond head hung in aggravation.

"You ok?" Rosemarie asked.

"Yeah, but I got to go. I have to be at briefing by 8:30, and I have to throw some stuff in my locker before that."

"Can I walk you to your car? You parked out back? Henry," she hollered to the back, "keep the bar under control? I'm going to step out back for a moment."

A tall, dark-haired man sauntered over. "Sure, Miss Lee," he answered.

Rosemarie threaded her arm through Matthew's as she escorted him through the rear of the building. Matthew wished they had walked out the front, so he could have spent more time with her.

They kissed goodbye, and Matthew drove off. Rosemarie leaned against the doorway and watched him leave, her heart full. Her previous boyfriend barely acknowledged her bar or how important her work was to her, and here was this guy she had known for less than two months asking to visit her at work, appreciating *Wine Time*.

Every time she was with Matthew, he made her feel significant, as if she mattered in the world and to him. She didn't know if it was possible to fall in love in so short a time, but she was definitely on her way with Matthew.

Rosemarie could not stop thinking about the impact of Matthew's visit. The more she contemplated, the more encouragement emanated from their relationship, and butterflies flitted around her chest at the thought of him. His strong shoulders and adorable dimples made her insides quiver whenever her thoughts drifted to him. His temperament and patience lit her up like she was high on a heady drug. Matthew was becoming her drug, and she was addicted. Making up her mind, she sent him a text.

Were you planning on meeting me for a run later tomorrow? She harbored a desire to match his boldness in her own, baby-steps style.

His text came back immediately. *Hey beautiful. I hope I can run with you tomorrow.*

She bit her lip, searching for the best way to word her next text. How much sleep would he need before their run? Would he be too worn out? Plotting a surprise sexual encounter, especially their first one, was not her forte. She tended to be a planner, but Matthew made her want to be impulsive.

Let's try for two pm for a run? Then, why don't you come by after? We can do a late lunch or early dinner post run at my house.

There, that sounded innocent enough.

Nine

Carter, of course, was always ecstatic to run, leaping and pulling on his lead, ready to go. Rosemarie joked the dog kept her honest in her running time. Matthew noticed his own running time increased when they ran with her dog, and now more than three months into his new, healthier lifestyle, he welcomed it. He never would keep up with the dog's full pace, but he felt faster and stronger than he had in a long time. Much of his extra flab around his middle had disappeared, his abs making their grand reappearance. He started lifting weights at home, and while he was far from a cover model, he enjoyed his more defined muscle tone. Just last night he flexed in front of the bathroom mirror, much to his own chagrin.

He caught Rosemarie glancing at his chest often, once while he was shirtless, her captivating eyes narrow and scorching. Her sly appreciation made all the work all the more worth it.

Their run ended at the entrance to the park, the heat of the afternoon growing more oppressive as the sun floated across the sky. The news predicted another heat wave for the upcoming week, and wiping sweat off his face with his shirt, Matthew did not deny it. Even poor Carter panted for more than normal, dog slobber dripping like a faucet, but with that same doggie smile plastered on his muzzle. Several sweat droplets rolled down Matthew's back, and he failed to consider was the sweaty mess he would be after the run. He would have to shower. At her house.

"Rosemarie, I am drowning in sweat. Do you want me to run home first to shower, then head over to your place?"

He rubbed his face again with his damp t-shirt as they walked back to her house, his hair sticking up in all directions.

She tilted her head toward him, her already dusky skin tanned from the sun and flushed from the run. She glowed like a Tuscan flower and gazed at him speculatively.

"You can shower at my place. I have clean towels."

She gave him a toothy grin, and he shrugged in consent. In truth, he was ecstatic to spend more time with her, even if he had to use her shower to do it. Showering at her place felt domestic, an exciting prospect with Rosemarie, and something he missed for a long time. Some people enjoy their time alone, but a gap had persisted in Matthew's life. He was not a man who wanted to live alone, and Rosemarie fit that gap to near perfection.

When she unlocked the front door to her small, rented ranch a block from the park, Carter vaulted to the large water bowl in the kitchen, creating a wet mess that resembled a water park. He then crept over to his dog bed, nuzzled his puppy toy ("his baby," Rosemarie called it), and collapsed on his side for a much-deserved nap. Rosemarie squatted down to pat the dog's fuzzy belly, then walked toward a short hall, flicking her head for Matthew to follow.

As she pulled a fluffy blue towel from the cabinet under the sink, she pointed out the showering amenities.

"Do you need more than shower gel and a shampoo/conditioner? I have more in my shower, if you need it."

Matthew smiled and shook his head.

Rosemarie's eyes popped open wide. "Oh!" she ducked back under the cabinet and extracted a red spray bottle which she set on the counter. "Deodorant. I collect all the free samples I can get, just in case."

Matthew raised an eyebrow. "Just in case," he repeated, no hiding the wry timbre of his voice. "No, this should be good," he assured her.

"OK then," she said stepping past him into the hall, the door clicking shut behind her. Then she raced to her bathroom to shower as quickly as she could.

Matthew was not the only one who had been hit by Cupid's arrow. Rosemarie's heart skipped throughout her chest at the thought of her man in uniform. She wanted to be sure he knew it.

❖ ❖

Matthew looked around the bathroom as he adjusted the water temperature. Compared to his spartan home interior, her rental was homey. He was no judge of design, but she seemed to have good taste. The bathroom had a beach theme, featuring large sea shells mounted on the wall.

He jumped into the shower, trying to be quick so he didn't keep her waiting, even though he was certain she was showering as well. After rinsing himself, he turned off the water and wiped down the shower with the towel. Only when he stepped out of the shower did he note that he had nothing to change into except his sweaty clothes presently in a heap on the bathroom counter. Sighing in defeat, he grabbed the dank tank top and shorts off the counter, cringing as he redressed.

He rubbed his hair dry, then hung the towel on a silver hook by the shower curtain, trying to leave the bath as neat as he found it. Having Rosemarie think he was a mess was not on his agenda for today. Matthew stepped into the hall, expecting to hear Rosemarie in the kitchen, but only silence welcomed him. Immediately on alert, he called out for her.

"In here."

Her voice carried down the hall. Changing directions, he walked farther down the hall and entered a pastel dream bedroom, complete with an exquisitely nude Rosemarie reclining on the pale teal bed. Matthew stopped short at the doorway, his heart beating in an erratic staccato.

Her damp hair formed a dark pool on the pillow, her black eyes smoldering and drawing him deep into the mystery of her. The light caramel tones of her skin stood in stark contrast to the colorful bedding. She was at the same time slender and curvy; her high, voluptuous breasts full, her toffee-colored nipples captivating. Her whole being called to him like a spell, like a tuning fork, an exotic enigma he wanted to spend the rest of his life solving. Matthew didn't bother to hide his thick erection obvious beneath his thin running shorts.

"Rosemarie," he broke the silence in a throaty voice. "Are you sure?"

He was almost afraid to ask. What he wanted was to jump on the bed, cover her completely, and shove his cock into her until he came in an explosive orgasm. What he needed, conversely, was her permission, her welcome. His fear of rushing in, of pushing her, held him at bay. He was almost afraid to touch her.

Rosemarie reached a slim hand toward him, her seductive smile inviting him to join her on the bed. She didn't need to say anything more. Matthew tugged his shirt over his head as he stepped into the room. Slipping his fingers into the waistband of his shorts, he paused with a raised eyebrow. Rosemarie nodded once, and he let the shorts fall, his manhood thrusting in front of him, a beacon seeking her.

Matthew slid onto the bed next to her, the cool movement of the fan helping to keep his overeager sweat at bay. She rolled to face him, clasping his face in her palm, tracing his eyebrows and nose with her thumb. His whole body melted into her touch.

She trailed her fingers down to his chest, tracing his chest muscles and the shadowy Marine insignia tattoo that covered most of his left pectoral. Rosemarie touched the tattoo with her tongue, and he shivered.

"Marine pride?" she asked, her eyes dancing.

"Ho-rah," Matthew replied in a husky tone. "Rosemarie —" he started, but she stopped his words with a kiss, her whole mouth taking his lips, her tongue probing for his.

He opened his mouth to take her in, playing his tongue against hers. He groaned deeply, and she took this as an invitation, pulling his muscled body over hers. Matthew did not hesitate to comply, moving between her silky golden thighs.

He reached between them with his hand, pressing his fingers to her velvety opening, and found her wet and waiting for him. He made to move down, to find her clit with his lips, but she clutched his arms, shifting him back up.

"Next time." Her whispers broke the stillness of the pastel afternoon. "I have been waiting too long already."

Matthew needed no added encouragement. He rose over her, his paler skin a contrast to her light bronze tones, and he could not keep his hands off her silky skin. Together they were night and day, dark and bright, ying and yang. Trailing his fingers over her hip, over her breasts, and across her collar bone, Matthew marveled at the softness he held.

He pressed into her lush opening, and her thighs clenched around his hips, pulling him in deeper. As he shuddered at the warm constriction of her pussy on his cock, the pleasure was pure and immediate. She traced her fingers over the muscles of his arm and grasped his hand, entwining her fingers with his. He captured her mouth in a soul-searching kiss.

At this moment, the world fell away as every inch of their skin touched, molded to one another, the intensity of their passion captivating him. Matthew had never felt so close, so entirely consumed, in his life. His member throbbed deeply as he hesitated, savoring the moment, hypnotized by the depth of her breathing and her musky sweet scent that rattled his senses. When he did move inside her mysterious depths, he was lost.

Rosemarie's entire body tingled at Matthew's touch, at once enthusiastic and gentle, as he tried to reign in his eagerness to better serve her. When he moved inside her, she sighed with the release of being fulfilled, his thickness surging deeper and deeper just as the weight of his body pressed down. Her world spun on its axis as she rocked in cadence with him. Matthew enveloped all of her, surrounded her, and she did not want that sensation to end.

Matthew worked his lips to capture hers, the tender pressure controlling the movements of his body within hers. He brushed at her taut nipples with his fingers, and she moaned at the gentle electric thrill. Her fingertips scorched his backside, and her clasping thighs forced him to focus before he came too fast. His internal conflict made his cock throb all the more — his body wanted to pound her into submission and hear her scream his name while his head and heart wanted to keep every motion pure and exquisite.

His lips traced a path from her mouth to her neck, allowing the undulation of her hips set the tone. His balls clenched against the base of his dick as his release built. Matthew reached his arm under Rosemarie's back to press her as close to him as possible, wanting every inch of his skin to touch hers.

Rosemarie gasped at the intimate pressure of his broad chest against her breasts, his lips on her neck. The pleasure that built inside her matched the frenzy of his body touching hers, his tongue on her ear, her name on his lips. Waves of ecstasy built deep within her core, searing her every nerve. She gripped his back trying to pull him impossibly closer and moaned his name. Her husky voice begging for him sent Matthew over the edge, and his thrusts became uncontrollable.

Together they abandoned the world as their passion consumed them, leaving them heaving and breathless on Rosemarie's sea foam-shaded bed in the muted afternoon light.

Rosemarie's face was flushed and relaxed when she finally roused herself, her satisfied gaze turning to Matthew. Those unfathomable black eyes pulled him in, and his desire to never leave her side inflamed within him.

Matthew's own Nordic eyes sparkled back at her, his burning blue heat holding her captive. Rosemarie lifted her hand to his face, capturing his dimpled cheek in her smooth palm. He pressed his head toward her hand, shifting his jaw to grace her palm with a feathery kiss. Her eyes crinkled at the movement, and she gave a yielding sigh at the sensation of his lips.

Her shimmery hair lay in ebony swirls across the pillows. Matthew wrapped a lock around his finger, a dark ring against his skin, and let the silkiness caress his hand. His eyes shifted to her hair as he played with it, then his icy intensity returned to her face.

"That was –" he began, his rough voice uncertain of what to say next.

"Amazing," Rosemarie finished for him. One of Matthew's eyebrows rose in a tawny arc.

"Unexpected," he countered.

A contented smile curved her mouth, and his eyes roved over her seductively.

"Well, that was part of my intent. You know how when you plan things, you can build them up in your head too much?"

Matthew nodded at the astuteness of her words. Encouraged, she continued.

"So, instead of telling you or setting up a big, elaborate date, I thought something basic for us, post-run, um, would take some of the pressure off."

"I can see that," Matthew conceded, then allowed his boyish smile to spread across his face. "But showering at your house was not exactly relaxing. I was so afraid I'd break your shower, or use the wrong towel, or —"

"The wrong towel?" Rosemarie's eyebrows furrowed like ravens' wings.

"I don't know," Matthew chuckled in response. "But do something wrong at your house."

Rosemarie threaded her elegant fingers together behind his head, pulling his face close to hers.

"You couldn't do anything wrong," she told him as she pressed his lips down to hers.

She allowed her tongue to play against his mouth, darting between his lips to electrify his tongue. The delicious taste of her tongue sent a jolt of excitement through Matthew, and his hands moved to her head, clutching at her hair as their lips explored each other.

Matthew pulled his head away, his ragged breath pulsing against her.

"Rosemarie, I feel like I can't stop when I'm with you. I want to be with you, touching you, hearing your voice, tasting your skin. I don't want you to think this is rushing, and I don't expect you to feel the same way. but can't imagine being without you."

He moved his hand from her hair to cup the delicate bones of her cheek. "I'm not an 'open my heart' kind of guy. I'm not sure what happened, but ever since I met you, my life has shifted on its foundations, and I don't want it to ever go back to the way it was."

He paused, his words hanging heavily in the dappled sunlight.

She did not miss the fear and uncertainty that painted his face as he spoke. Matthew may not have known it, but her own heart mirrored his words. Rosemarie was used to being guarded, even with her ex, so having Matthew open his heart to her, to lay his emotions at her feet, loosened the tension she that had built inside.

She trailed a fingernail down his nose. He snatched his mouth forward to capture her fingertip in his teeth, lightening the mood.

"I don't feel rushed," she confirmed.

Ten

T he time he spent with Rosemarie went by in a blur. Matthew tried to spend every spare minute with her. They continued taking Carter running; she made him dinner one night, a superb Eggplant Parmesan that would rival the best chefs in the country.

"Don't make this again," he told her, shoveling another mouthful in, "otherwise you will see what I looked like several months ago. I do not want that body back."

She had giggled at the compliment. She also admitted that she did not cook often and told him to enjoy while it was here.

His favorite moments with her, however, were the low-key nights when they didn't work — Mondays and Tuesdays — when they sat on the couch, ate popcorn or a charcuterie platter, and watched television together.

Matthew hated to tell her he preferred B-rated action films, and her laugh tinkled like a wind chime at his confession.

"What, the ones with bad dialog and washed up movie stars?" Her eyebrows reached her hairline as she asked.

Matthew shook his head, his cheeks flushed. "I know it's bad, but I don't have to think while I watch them, and they are so funny."

Rosemarie could not stop the wide grin that spread across her face. "Well, I don't have a strong preference for films either way. I'll watch anything, so if you want to watch aging movie stars try to build up their bank accounts before they have to quit acting altogether, we can do that."

She patted his knee as she spoke while he reached his head over the popcorn bowl to kiss her buttery lips.

"I feel so indulged, like a spoiled little kid," he joked.

"Oh, you should," she joked back. "I'll find some way for you to make it up to me."

The dark pools of her eyes glistened with suggestion. Matthew's grin matched her smile, and she cuddled into him, hitting "play" on the remote.

When movie nights went late (as they typically did), Rosemarie still went home if they were at Matthew's. Although the oversized screen made for great viewing, someone had to be home with Carter. Rosemarie had not taken Matthew up on his offer to bring the dog over. She always invited Matthew to stay with her if the movie nights were at her place; at first, he turned her down, feeling it was perhaps too soon or inappropriate. After the third time he tried, she pressed the issue.

"Matthew, I don't feel rushed," she told him flatly. "I'm not asking you to move in. Hell, I won't even offer to make you breakfast. But I would like you in bed with me."

"You were going to offer breakfast?" His eyes widened, feigning devastation. She elbowed him in return. "How about I make breakfast in the morning?" Matthew offered, leaning in closer.

His implication sent a surge of excitement flooding through her. She placed her dainty hand behind his neck to pull his face near hers. Her heart thundered against her breast, and she could see that Matthew's chest heaved in cadence to hers. She lifted his hand, slipping it under her shirt to cup her full breast. Matthew moved his thumb over the lace of her bra, his cock clenching as her nipple hardened at his touch.

He slipped his hand down her waist to the vee of her legs, cupping her pussy through the thin fabric of her leggings. He moved his finger back and forth, alternating pressure in response to her moaning. Rosemarie let her head fall back and her legs splay farther apart as his fingers danced between her legs. She wanted more. She wanted his tongue on her clit. She wanted him all.

Rosemarie snaked her hand to the front of Matthew's pants, squeezing his package under the dense fabric of his jeans, and he groaned.

"Do you make eggs?" she asked before kissing him with a desperate, inner hunger, and crushing into each other, they stumbled toward her bedroom.

Meeting her parents for the first time caught him by surprise.

He left early for work on a Wednesday night with a plan of tucking a sappy card into Rosemarie's screen before he meandered to the station and began his shift for the week. He wore his clean uniform since it was the first night back, and he felt grateful his vest and belt were in his locker at the station. Sweat droplets already populated across his forehead — wearing the vest and belt would only make the stifling heat worse. Perhaps the heat would keep the criminal element at bay; it was too freaking *hot* to mess around.

Sunset cast Rosemarie's street into warm tones of auburn and gold, the uber-bright light forcing him to squint against the glare. That same glaring brightness reflected off Rosemarie's car still sitting in her driveway. Flicking his eyes to the clock on his dash, his brows pulled together. *Why was she still home? Was she sick?* He wracked his brain, trying to recall if she had told him she wasn't going into work today.

He pulled behind a bland silver sedan on the street and rushed to the door, his card looking worse for wear as he clutched it in his anxious palm. His officer persona overtook him as he stepped up to the tiny porch and rapped smartly on the door. It took everything he had not to follow the action with "Tustin Police."

Rosemarie pulled the door open, a laugh on her face, responding to someone speaking inside. Carter leapt to her side, excited to see who was at the door. Rosemarie's face alighted with delight when she found Matthew standing on her porch.

"Matthew! Is everything OK? You look great in uniform!" she fairly squealed, one eye winking in suggestive glee.

"Yeah, no. I was coming by leave this in your door," he held out the now-grimy card, and Rosemarie's onyx eyes widened. "But you are home ..." his words trailed off as he tipped his head to the side to peer around her. His face was closed with firm intensity, evaluating the situation as though he was on patrol.

Rosemarie's laughter bubbled up as she opened the screen for him. "Oh, Matthew, I thought I said something, but maybe I didn't? I think I mentioned how my parents and I try to get together for dinner two or three times a month? Well, they asked if I would take this Wednesday off for dinner, and I decided my crew could handle the bar until I got there later."

She scrolled her eyes up and down his uniform-clad form. As she did, two people came up behind her to satiate their curiosity at the door. Rosemarie's parents.

Matthew's chest sunk to his feet. He had no idea this was dinner night, and here he was invading, wearing his uniform no less, which did not always send the best message, and he had no time to prepare for meeting the 'rents.

Holy bad timing, Batman, he thought.

"Why don't you come in," she offered, and how could he say no? Other than the obvious *I got to get to work* cop-out, and Rosemarie knew what time he normally left for work. She knew he still had an extra half hour. Plus, he was not about to start lying to her, or her parents, especially over something as trivial as an accidental meeting with her parents. Time to man up. He plastered what he hoped was a winning smile across his face as stepped through the door, handing the card to Rosemarie and wiping his nervous hands on his pants.

Mr. Lee was tall and slender with wavy walnut hair and a firm grip when he shook Matthew's hand; however, with Mrs. Lee, Matthew could see where Rosemarie got her dark beauty. Mrs. Lee was as tiny and energetic as a fitful bird, obviously thrilled to finally meet the man in her daughter's life. Maybe the uniform worked to his advantage; Mrs. Lee did not stop fawning over him as they sat at the table for dinner.

And while it appeared Matthew won over Rosemarie's mother (who rested her hand lightly on his shoulder every time she spoke to him), Mr. Lee seemed reticent, cautious, of course, over this strange man dating his daughter. Matthew's discomfort was evident from his ramrod straight back and tense jaw.

Sitting down to dinner in full uniform was not the way he wanted to meet Rosemarie's parents. At least he didn't have a gun strapped to his hip. What impression would *that* have made?

Since Matthew had to eat quickly and leave for his shift, Rosemarie served him a small plate. She and her mother kept up most of the conversation, letting him focus on his meal. Swallowing was difficult, as Mr. Lee's silent scrutiny never left Matthew.

Mrs. Lee's fawning more than made up for her silent husband, and when Matthew finished, she rushed to clear his plate and escort him to the door. Rosemarie and Mr. Lee followed. Mrs. Lee enclosed him in a hug that seemed too large for her small frame. Matthew could not help but hug her back.

"It was so great to meet you, Matthew! Rosemarie has talked about you so much, I needed to put a face to all those compliments!" she gushed.

"Mother," Rosemarie's exasperation showed in her voice. She shrugged an apology toward Matthew who gave her a compassionate grin in return. His expression told her *Moms, what can you do?*

Then Mr. Lee approached him, and Matthew stiffened. He had not made a good impression on Rosemarie's father, and Matthew cringed at the thought of what Mr. Lee's parting words may be.

In a move that shocked Matthew, Mr. Lee pressed forward, clasped Matthew's hand in a farewell handshake, then pulled Matthew into a half hug with his left arm. Matthew's sky-blue eyes were wide with astonishment. Mr. Lee put his face close to Matthew's.

"Be safe out there. My daughter cares for you." Mr. Lee patted Matthew's back and stepped back to his wife.

Matthew prided himself on not being caught off-guard often, but Mr. Lee had done just that. He gave Rosemarie a sidelong glance of utter disbelief. She giggled through pursed lips and threaded her arm through Matthew's, walking him out the door and closing it behind her. She wanted no peepers watching them on the porch.

"So, a card?" she asked, one raven's wing eyebrow raised. Matthew blushed to the roots of his hair.

"It's just a funny card – about running with a dog. I was at the grocery and saw it on some end-cap and had to get it."

The endearing nature of his gesture was like his hand cupping her heart. Rosemarie could not stop the flattered grin that spread across her face.

"I love that you wanted to drop it off. Sorry to spoil the surprise."

She reached up, wrapping her hand around the heated skin of his neck. Matthew followed the pull of her hand, leaning in to touch his lips to hers. He pressed his tongue past her parted lips, and his own heart raced as his tongue explored hers.

Rosemarie wanted to lose herself in that kiss, but in the back of her mind, the reminder of where they were forced her to halt. Her parents, his job, outside on her porch — this was not the time or place to let the fire for him consume her.

Matthew was consumed, and he forgot where he was until she pressed her dainty hands against his uniformed chest. He pulled back, exhaling heavily.

"Maybe save the rest for later this week?" he suggested. Rosemarie allowed her fingers to play with the seams of his navy-blue shirt.

"That is a guarantee," she told him. Matthew gave her one more quick kiss on her cheek before jumping down the porch stairs.

It was not long before their not-rushed relationship turned into something more serious.

Matthew woke with Rosemarie's hair tangled around his arm, her firm backside pressing against Matthew's hip. He shifted so as not to wake her with his early morning hard on. Morning sunlight managed to pierce her room-darkening drapes, the same type that hung in his bedroom — a standard for those who worked nights, he presumed. The rays avoided her eyes but alighted on her shoulders and the side swells of her breast, and he could not tear his gaze from her. Garza had joked earlier that his romance was a whirlwind, but Matthew had known her for several months now, and every day with her made him happier than the last.

His staring must have alerted her on a subconscious level. Rosemarie blinked her eyes open and focused them on Matthew's cerulean gaze. She blew him a kiss with a moue of her lips, then licked her dry lips.

"What are you doing, babe?" Her usually silky voice came out in a croaky morning whisper.

"I was just looking at you and thinking."

"What are you thinking?" she asked, one side of her lip turned up in encouragement.

He absently twirled a lock of her hair in his finger as he considered his words.

"I don't want you to think this is rushing —" he started, and she barked out a laugh, placing a finger over his mouth.

"I'm not rushing, remember?"

"Ok," he said in a rush of breath, "Rosemarie, I want to tell you that the last few months have been amazing. I didn't know life could feel this way. I —" he paused a moment, and Rosemarie's eyebrows knitted in confusion.

"Are you breaking up with me?"

"What? NO!" Matthew's voice was both commanding and comforting. He grasped her hand in his large, calloused one. "The opposite! I wanted to say—" again he paused. His mind reeled with the seriousness of what he felt and what he wanted – no, needed – to say to this woman who had changed his world.

"Holy shit, Matthew, you just better say it. You are killing me with all this."

"I love you, Rosemarie," he finally blurted out.

Rosemarie stilled, her heart fluttering as she fought the swell of emotions that cascaded inside her. His admission of love, readily expressed in his eyes that remained focused on hers, released a sense of completeness, a fulfillment she didn't know she missed. And she admired him for putting it out there when he had to be uncertain how she would respond.

Her whole face relaxed, and she pushed herself up on her elbow so her gaze met his, dark water meeting ocean blue. At once she knew. She knew like she knew her own name, her own mind. Everything in her life had led her to this moment: a quiet morning in a soft bed with a man who loved her.

"Oh, Matthew," she breathed, placing her hand on the stubble of his jaw. "I love *you*. I've been a bit scared to open myself too much, but everywhere I turned, you were there. Supportive, caring, encouraging, and my heart just opened without my say so."

She leaned forward to kiss him, and he quivered at the pressure of her lips and the meaning of her words.

"I was afraid you would be more hesitant, what with your divorce and all. I was afraid I would be rushing *you*!"

Matthew's face softened in understanding. "Is that why you kept telling me 'I'm not rushed'?" He clapped his hand against his forehead. "I get it now."

Rosemarie gave him a grin full of opportunity and suggestion.

"Well, not yet. Do you want to get some before we leave the bed?"

Matthew did not hesitate, but rolled on top of her, his morning hard-on aggressively probing. His lips parted hers in a soul-searching kiss, one filled with passion, hope, and possibility.

Eleven

A relatively quiet late fall evening is not welcome on the night shift, as it is a harbinger of chaos. While the shocking heat had cooled, the air still held the warmth of the day. As if dispatch heard Matthew's thoughts, the radio squawked to life.

"T44, you copy?"

Matthew distractedly reached for the button on his radio, his other hand tapping notes into his onboard computer. "T44, copy."

"T44, we have a suspect on the run. Domestic. White male, 20s, brown hair and eyes, light t-shirt and jeans, last seen running down Warner Avenue. Witnesses say the suspect has a gun. No shots fired reported."

"10-4, enroute. Copy."

Matthew hit his lights and blinker, flipped the car around, and headed back toward Warner Street.

Approaching the area indicated, he cut his lights and siren, weaving up and back through the subdivision where dispatch reported the perp was last seen. The suspect was reputed to be high and had beat up his girlfriend. A knowing awareness crept over him, and Matthew radioed dispatch for the girlfriend's name.

"Reporting party gives her name as Denise Miscula."

"Fuck," Matthew cussed in a low voice.

The perp currently on the run was the same naked, sweaty, son of a bitch he had to tackle to the ground months ago. *How did the fucker make bail?* Matthew searched the yards as he drove.

The houses in this neighborhood were like dark monoliths, everyone inside either asleep or getting ready for bed, reverse animals hibernating from the dull heat. No neighborhood parties, no open garages. It was still too freaking stifling to be awake, even at night.

Not seeing anything amiss in the subdivision, Matthew worked his way toward the main streets. Matthew expected the guy would try to break into a closed business — at 1:30 am, few places were open, and most businesses did not have great security. As he turned onto Warner, his radio beeped into his earpiece again. This time it was Ramon Garza.

"Danes, I have eyes on the perp. Warner and Wright."

Warner and Wright? A sudden, sinking sensation rippled through Matthew's gut. Stepping on the gas, he kept the car silent and grappled with his radio button. Years of experience taught him to manage fear and panic, but the cross-streets from Garza bit him harshly. He pressed the radio button.

"Which direction, Garza? Which direction, on Wright?"

"South."

Matthew's heart fell into the pit in his stomach as he hit the lights and siren full blast. He couldn't call 99 on the radio yet; he wasn't certain that the perp was headed for the only open business on Wright, but life had a way of biting him in the ass.

Matthew saw Garza's lights on the black and white, the 12-vehicle empty. Garza was approaching on foot. The lights for *Wine Time* were the only other color emblazoned against the evening sky, just inside the city limits.

"What's your ten-twenty, Garza?" Matthew asked into his radio as he leapt out of his vehicle, unclipping his gun as he advanced on the businesses on the west side. Tyrell was enroute but needed to cover some distance as he raced from the east side of town.

"Back of the strip mall. I saw him race toward here, but I'm not seeing or hearing him. Go around front, brother."

"Copy," Matthew responded and drew his weapon.

The elegant door to *Wine Time* was slightly ajar, but no sound drifted out. For this late on a Saturday night, music, conversation, the tinkling of glassware, some sounds should have escaped. The silence alone was as telling as any noise the perp could make. Matthew tipped his head close to his radio.

"1-2, I have an open bar door, seems to be the only business open on the street, but no noise from inside. Cover me from the back."

"Copy," Garza squawked via the radio.

Matthew eased his line of sight around the open door, his back against the door frame. Several wine bottles dripping scarlet and clear broken glass littered the smooth wood floor. The entry was otherwise empty. Stepping lightly on his toes into the front entryway, he tried to avoid crunching the broking glass under his boots and strained to hear any noise from the main room of the bar.

The drugged-up perp barked out a command which was followed squealing. Matthew followed the sound to the arched entry to the main bar. Keeping himself hidden in the shadow of the doorway, he scanned the scene. A few employees and several customers hid behind the booths as a gunman matching the perp's description waved a Smith and Wesson 9 mil in his sweaty hand. The perp's dark brown hair looked almost oily, pasted onto his head, and his back was to Matthew.

Looking past the 9-mil into the bar proper, Matthew could see Rosemarie's hooded eyes peek up past the few remaining upright wine bottles on the bar counter. The perp seemed ignorant of the weapon in his own hand or that he was threatening people with it. He appeared confused and disturbed, and Matthew was relieved no one was in the man's sights.

Rosemarie's eyes latched onto Matthew's, her ever-delicate eyebrows rising in surprise. Matthew held one finger to his lips in a silent shushing gesture, and she scrunched lower below the counter. He needed to keep the aim of the gun away from that bar at all costs.

Stealthy and light, Matthew managed to step out of the perp's line of sight, and the gunman was unaware of his presence. Sweat soaked the perp's t-shirt. Matthew surmised the perp was as high as a kite again and prepared himself for another moist wrestling match *if* he could get the suspect the drop the gun. Just as Matthew was about to identify himself, a voice from the left of the bar called out.

"This is the police! Drop the gun and put your hands in the air! You are under arrest!" Garza's commanding voice diverted the gunman's attention.

As the perp shifted his body, and the 9 mil with him, toward Garza's voice, Matthew slipped smoothly behind him, like a dancer on a stage, and clasped the man's gun in his right hand, forcing it toward the ceiling. Deftly, he wrapped his left arm around the man's neck into a chokehold. The gunman released the gun, trying to use both hands to dislodge Matthew's iron grip.

Garza ran up, his gun trained on the perp, as Matthew wrestled the man to the ground in the vice-like hold. The gunman's struggles lessened as Garza intoned, "You have the right to remain silent. Anything you say can be used against you in a court of law. You have the right to an attorney —"

"You can stop," Matthew told him, lifting his arms from the perp's neck. The sleeper hold worked; the perp lay motionless and damp, the chest of his dingy, wet shirt rising and falling in a steady cadence. Garza punched Matthew on the shoulder.

"You solid?" Garza asked. Matthew nodded, trying to slow his heart after the adrenaline rush of taking down an intoxicated gunman in a hostage situation.

"Yeah, brother. You?"

"Always," Garza said as he pulled out a rubber glove, intent on retrieving the gun that lay on the ground not far from the sleeping perp.

Settling his gun back in the holster and snapping the hood to secure his weapon, Matthew worked his way amid the chaos to the bar. His attention never wavered from the dark, panicked eyes that barely rose above the counter. More sirens echoed in the distance, announcing the cavalry had arrived. The wine bar was about to be busier at two am than it had ever been before.

Matthew stepped nimbly around the counter to find Rosemarie crouched low, only the top of her sable hair peeking above the countertop. When she saw Matthew, she stood, her limbs visibly shaking. Matthew moved to her, wrapping her in his strong embrace, her cheek pressing against the rough polyester of his uniform. The panic of a wild gunman dissipated, and she collapsed into him, her strong runner's legs for once unable to support her weight.

He placed a hand on Rosemarie's head, stroking her silky hair to calm her. A few cuts on her forehead and arms from broken glass bled, dripping onto her brilliant white shirt and getting lost in the navy blue of his uniform. A flare of anger burst through him, that this high, crazed lunatic could have hurt someone one he loved so dearly, and he had to physically restrain himself from racing back over to the perp and kicking him in the face. Instead, he flicked his radio on with his free hand to request ambulance assistance, for both Rosemarie and the perp, and anyone else who may have been injured.

After Tryell arrived with another unit, the lights and sirens illuminated the night like a carnival. The paramedics arrived shortly after and began assessing the injured. Matthew escorted a dazed Rosemarie to the ambulance, anxious to remain by her side. Once she was under the care of the paramedics outside, he promised he would be back to take her home, then re-entered the chaos inside her wine bar.

Ramon had the perp locked in the back of his car already, well away from the fury blazing beneath Matthew's skin. He and Tyrell were in the miserable throes of taking witness statements, and they all dreaded the paperwork that would follow this mess.

"What are the odds he would make it all the way here. To your girlfriend's wine shop?" Garza asked, perplexed.

Matthew shook his head, his own disbelief showing on his face.

"At least we got him, brother," Garza continued, his voice smooth and reassuring.

Twelve

Fortunately, the paramedics gave everyone, include Rosemarie, a clean bill of health that night. While they would wear the cuts and scratches as badges of honor for a week or two, the scrapes would heal, leaving only faint scars, if any, of this misadventure. The emotional scars, however, would take much longer to mend.

After three in the morning, as the bedlam wore down, most of the witnesses and first responders departed. Only Garza remained with Matthew and Rosemarie, who stared around her beloved wine bar, her face a stunned mask at the damage. Glass crunched under Ramon's boots as he stepped closer to Rosemarie.

"The good news, if there can be any, is that most of this looks superficial. At least the guy didn't take out a wall or something." He flicked his sage eye to Matthew before continuing. "This is the type of job that really just needs cleanup. A bunch of us are off tomorrow and Monday. Why don't we all come down and help clean up?"

Rosemarie's zombie-like gaze barely registered his offer. All she could do was rotate her head around her beloved bar. Matthew clasped her hands in his gentle fingers, encouraging her to concentrate on him.

"Rosemarie, baby? You Ok?"

Her eyes searched erratically at first, then landed on Matthew's earnest face. The lines around his mouth showed the strain of the night and his concern for her. Matthew may be accustomed to crazed gunmen, but Rosemarie was not. He must remind himself of that.

"Rosemarie? Why don't we leave this for tonight? I'll have the officers lock up, and I'll take you home."

"I don't want to go home." Her flat voice matched her eyes. Matthew's brow furrowed at her.

"I think you should, baby," he told her, his tone low, supportive. "I think —"

"I don't want to go home." Her voice raised an octave. Matthew panicked. Perhaps she was in shock?

"Ok, but you can't stay here. Where do you want to go?"

"I don't want to go home!" Rosemarie's whole body clenched, and Matthew reacted, enclosing her in his muscled embrace.

"OK. OK," was all he could come up with, and he cast a desperate look at Garza.

"Hey, brother," Garza also kept his voice low, like they were trying to calm a skittish horse. "How about we write this up, and you take her to your place? Maybe she needs someone to stay with her? Unless, her parents?"

Contacting her parents would have to happen, but not at three in the morning. Calls about raving gunmen were not well received in the middle of the night. Their daughter was fine, and Matthew needed to keep centered on Rosemarie. Garza was right. She needed someone to make her feel safe and protected, and Matthew was more than willing to serve that role for her. He nodded toward Garza.

"Thank you, brother. I'll text you tomorrow morning, meet you all here?"

Garza waved Matthew off. "Whatever, brother. Just go take care of her."

Keeping Rosemarie in the fold of his arm, he stepped forward, escorting her over the scatter of broken glass that clinked and crunched under the heavy pressure of his boots. The lights of the police cars out front continued to flare, and they walked out the door into a dizzying disco of red and blue strobe.

Matthew clasped Rosemarie tighter to keep her upright as they approached his black and white. She remained wordless as he placed her in the passenger seat of the car, then he slid into the driver's seat to take her home. To his home.

Matthew had to swap cars at the station, and Rosemarie was uncomfortably quiet the whole time. Filling the air with useless conversation felt inappropriate, so he let the deafening silence permeate the car as he drove home.

They were near his street when he realized she would probably need some items from her house. Flipping the car in a sharp U-turn, he sped to her place and asked her to stay in the car as he ran inside. When he opened the door, Carter barked in surprise, then bowled him off balance trying to get attention. He gave the beast an obligatory pat on the head as he walked down the hall, grabbing Rosemarie's toothbrush from her bathroom, a t-shirt she had thrown over the end of her bed, Carter's dog bed and leash, and the canister of dog food from the pantry. Carter wagged his entire furry body as Matthew clipped the leash to his collar and led the dog outside.

"Sorry, boy," Matthew told the dog, "No run right now."

Juggling everything and the dog's leash, he struggled to open the door to the back seat of the car. Carter needed no encouragement and hopped in, licking at Rosemarie as he settled down. Matthew tucked the rest of the items in the back pocket of the front seat, scratched his fingers through Carter's thick fur once more, then took the driver's seat and resumed the drive back to his house.

Rosemarie came to life when Carter entered the car. Her dog continued to nose at her, licking her cheek and hair as though he knew she needed the attention.

"You got Carter?" She faced Matthew as he drove, her eyes full of tears. *That was the reason for the silence,* Matthew thought. *She was trying not to cry.*

"Of course, I got Carter, babe. We can't leave him all night by himself." His lips tugged into a small smile at her. "We may work the night shift, but your boy doesn't. He would have gone crazy waiting for you."

Rosemarie rested her hand on the dog's head and leaned toward Matthew.

"Thank you, Matthew. Thank you—"

"You don't need to thank me," he interrupted. "I was just . . ." His voice trailed off.

"You were not going to say, 'doing your job,' were you, Officer Danes?"

Matthew dropped his eyes as a flush rose from the collar of his uniform.

"That's not what I was thanking you for, babe," she explained. "Thank you for taking care of me. For thinking of Carter, that I would need him tonight, for taking me to your house. Thank you for being the man I need."

Matthew bit his lip and swallowed hard. The road blurred in front of him, and he blinked several times to clear his vision. He pulled into his driveway and put the car in park. Lifting his finger in a mock tip of a hat, he bowed his head at Rosemarie.

"At your service, ma'am."

Matthew left Carter in the living room to nose around as he helped Rosemarie change into the t-shirt he grabbed from her room and a clean pair of his sweatpants. Once in comfy clothes, he tucked her into his bed, and tossed her white work shirt into the washing machine on cold, uncertain if stain would come out. Making the hard decision to throw the shirt away if it did not come out clean, he entered the living room to find Carter standing near the doorway of the hall, a subtle whining emanating from the depths of his woolly chest.

He stroked the dog on his head and unclipped the dangling leash.

"Come 'ere, boy." He called the dog into the kitchen to get the dog food and water bowls set up on the tile floor at the end of the counter. Carter lapped at the water twice, before lifting his dripping head to continue his whining. Matthew knelt to rub the dog's head between his hands.

"I know, boy. You are worried about her. She's OK." Matthew rose, scooped up Carter's bedding, and headed down the hall. Carter stopped at the archway to the hall, his ears high.

"It's *OK*," Matthew told the dog as he patted his thigh. "You can come here."

With mincing steps, Carter walked down the hallway toward the bedroom. The dog's dark head went right to Rosemarie's hair, and he licked at her head. Carter studied Matthew as he adjusted the dog bed on the floor between the dresser and the closet, within close view of Rosemarie. Carter tottered over to his bed and stepped onto it delicately, then collapsed his dense body on the bedding and rested his head on his paws, ready for sleep.

"You would think your night was as busy as ours, lazy dog," Matthew whispered.

His fingers found the zipper to his uniform shirt easily in the dim light. The ripping sound of his bulletproof vest, however, was a shock in the peaceful air of the room. Carter emitted a short yelp in response, and Rosemarie's head popped out from under the covers.

"Sorry," he told her.

"No, no sorry," she answered as she resettled in the bed. "It's a good sound. It means you are home safe."

Before she let sleep overcome her, she flipped back the coverlet on his side of the bed in invitation. Matthew reveled in a moment of realization. This is how his life – their life – would be. Rosemarie in his bed, awaiting him, happy, secure, complete, their dog reclining within view. This was the home his heart had craved.

He stepped into the small excuse of a walk-in closet and stripped off the rest of his uniform, hung it on the closet door, then slipped into a pair of sweats himself.

As he re-entered the bedroom, a sense of contentment settled into his chest. Tomorrow he would have to call her parents, assure them Rosemarie was safe, then go with her to the wine bar and begin cleaning up the mess so she could resume her life. Her life with him.

But that was tomorrow. Tonight, they would sleep together. He would hold her throughout the night, keeping her safe, his arms reassuring her that whatever the future held, they would face it together.

Even after the miserable pandemonium of the day, he climbed into bed happy and wrapped himself around Rosemarie's slender length, allowing himself to melt into her, blissful sleep enveloping them both.

An Excerpt from *Day Shift* –

Ramon Garza rolled over, rubbing the sand out of his eyes, cringing at the sounds that permeated his bedroom door and filled his ears, waking him from an already rough sleep.

He loved his kids, his family, honestly, he did. At least that is what he told himself in a mantra to help him gear up and face the day. His eyes did not cooperate — they did not even want to open. He held over on patrol the night before, coming home two hours later than normal, then had to help with the kids and crashed hard when his head hit the pillow. He hoped for a full night's sleep, but here it was, not even 6 am, and it sounded like all three kids were awake. Why was the baby howling?

Garza's move from the night shift to the day shift had been a struggling transition. He found it difficult to fall asleep at night and wake up early enough to make it to briefing. And that was if the baby slept all night and did not wake up him every two hours. Ramon pressed his palms to his eyes. How did he and Jazmin do this with the other two kids? He didn't recall it being this hard. Or maybe he was getting too old?

A loud crash sent the baby into another squealing howl, and Ramon jumped up, threw on a t-shirt, and left the sanctuary of his bedroom.

The kitchen island opened into a wide living room, and the entire area looked as though a tornado rampaged through. Clothes and towels were draped over the back of the couch and the island bar chairs. Toys littered the floor so much that Ramon had to pick his way around the clutter, the world's worst obstacle course. Ramon would have rather competed in the police training course than walk through his own home. The chaos of his home weighed heavily on his chest.

His chest only sunk lower into the pit of his belly when he gazed at his wife, and he hated himself for the thoughts that passed through his mind. Jasmine was still a beautiful woman, just not the beautiful woman he married. Her normally styled hair hung in limp waves around her face. A matching set of luggage hugged her eyes, even as she sat in a daze staring at the TV, hugging the baby in her arms as the two other kids ran around like savages. She had not changed out of her pajamas and robe for the last several days while he was on shift. He could not judge her, he knew, with but the trials of work, kids, the house, and Ramon dreamed of the days when they were first married, no kids, no worries, and Jasmine was his hot young wife.

A Thank You to My Readers –

I would like to extend a heartfelt thank you to all of you for taking a chance and reading this new series. Even with some extensive writing experience – including teaching others how to write! – actually completing a novel and publishing it involves the writer opening herself up, exposing herself in way that is challenging. That you, dear reader, took the chance to read this romantic tale makes the risk worth it.

I would also like to thank my kids and family in general for always supporting me. They always assumed writing was my real job. To my encouraging children, Mommy has always been an author. And my mom, who saw her daughter get a degree in English, of all things, and made no judgements, and instead remained confident that her daughter would be successful even with such an inauspicious field of study.

Finally, I would like to thank Michael, the man in my life who has been so supportive of my career shift to focus more on writing, and who makes a great sounding board for ideas. He is also my hero in blue, and I listen for that sound of his safe return home every night.

If you liked this book, please leave a review! Reviews can be bread and butter for an author, and I appreciate your comments and feedback!

About the Author

Michelle Deerwester-Dalrymple is a professor of writing and an author. She started reading when she was 3 years old, writing when she was 4, and published her first poem at age 16. She has written articles and essays on a variety of topics, including several texts on writing for middle and high school students. Her books include The Glen Highland Romance series: *To Dance in the Glen, The Lady of the Glen*, soon to be followed by the third: *The Exile of the Glen.* She is presently working on a novel inspired by actual events, which she hopes to release by the end of 2019. She lives in California with her family of seven.

Amazon Author page: https://www.amazon.com/-/e/B07C784SJ6
You can visit her blog page and sign up for her newsletter at:
https://michelledeerwesterdalrympleauthor.blogspot.com/

Follow her on
On Facebook: https://www.facebook.com/MDDauthor/

On Instagram:
https://www.instagram.com/michelledalrympleauthor/

On Twitter: https://twitter.com/mddalrymple

On Pinterest: https://www.pinterest.com/lamuse99/

Made in the USA
Columbia, SC
31 October 2020